characters created by lauren child

YOU can be my friend

PUFFIN

Text based on the script written by Carol Noble

Illustrations from the TV animation
produced by Tiger Aspect

PUFFIN BOOKS
Published by the Penguin Group: London, New York, Australia,
Canada, India, Ireland, New Zealand and South Africa
Penguin Books Ltd, Registered Offices: 80 Strand, London WC2R 0RL, England

puffinbooks.com

This edition published in Great Britain in Puffin Books 2010
1 3 5 7 9 8 6 4 2
Text and illustrations copyright © Lauren Child / Tiger Aspect Productions Limited, 2008
The Charlie and Lola Logo is a trademark of Lauren Child
All rights reserved. The moral right of the author/illustrator has been asserted
Manufactured in China
ISBN: 978-0-141-33494-3
This edition produced for The Book People Ltd,
Hall Wood Avenue, Haydock, St Helens, WA11 9UL

I have this little sister Lola.
She is small and very funny.
Today Lola is excited because
Marv is coming over and he is
bringing his little brother Morten.

Lola says,
"Me and Morten
are going to do
LOTS of things together,
like have a tea party!

I LOVE having tea parties.
And dressing up!
Everyone LOVES
dressing up."

Then I say,
"If you run out
of things to do,
Morten really likes playing
Round-and-Round."

But Lola says,
        "Oh no!
I really do not like
        Round-and-Round.

All you do is
        go round
and round...
        and round.
Nothing happens, Charlie."

Then the doorbell rings
        and Lola shouts,
"MORTEN'S HERE!"

Lola says,
  "Hello, Morten."

Morten doesn't
  say **anything**.

So Marv says,
  "Morten's not really
a big talker."

        And Lola says,
"Morten, do you
    want to see my room?"

But Morten still
    doesn't say **anything**.

Lola says,
    "Would you like
a cup of tea, Morten?"

Morten just stares.

    So then she asks,
"Would you like a biscuit?"

Not a peep from Morten.

"Oh," says Lola.
"Well, what we'll
        do now is...

"... **dressing** up!
Look at me, Morten.
I'm a mermaid.

Morten, you can be
a **pirate**."

But Morten
    just stands there.

So Lola says,
        "I know!
Let's pretend we live
        in **Upside Down**."

Lola says,
"In Upside Down,
        absolutely everything
is completely
            ¡uʍop ǝpᴉsdn

    Would you like
a tea of cup, Morten?
            That's Upside Down
for 'cup of tea'!"

Morten doesn't even move.

    So Lola shouts,
"Morten! Don't you
            want to play?"

Morten just shakes his head.

Later, Lola whispers,
    "Morten didn't like
any of my games, Charlie.
        He didn't even
    talk to me."

So I say,
    "Marv told you,
Morten isn't really
            a big talker."

Then Lola says,
    "But he didn't even
say one SINGLE word.
        He doesn't like me."

    Then Lola sighs
            and blows some
bubbles in her pink milk.

And do you know what?
Morten starts giggling.

"Hee hee hee hee hee hee."

Then Morten tries blowing
pink milk bubbles.

Lola and Morten
giggle some more.

Then Lola says,
"I know! I know!
Next let's play
bubbles outside.

Morten, what do you
think it would be like
to be inside a bubble?"

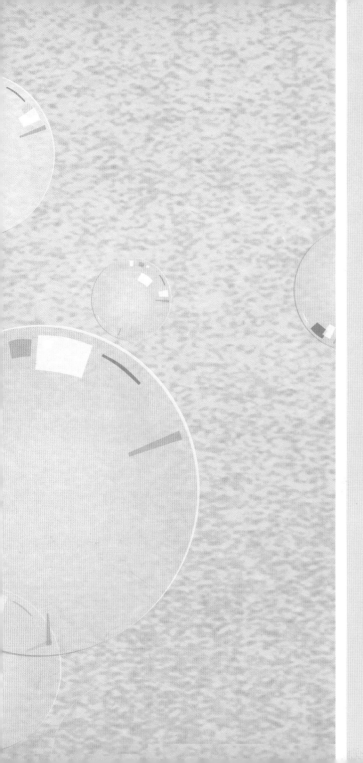

"Bubbly," says Morten.

"I looooove
being in a bubble,"
			says Lola.

And Morten says,
"I love being
			in a bubble, too."

Later, we all have
        tea at Marv and
Morten's flat.
            Lola and Morten
can't stop **giggling** and
        whispering together.

        Morten asks,
"Would you like to
        play a game, Lola?
It's called
        Round-and-Round!"

        Lola looks unsure
so I say, "Go on, Lola."

And Lola says,
        "OK, Charlie. But only
because Morten is my
        new special **friend**."

Morten says,
"Your turn, Lola! What you do is…"
"I know," says Lola. "You go rOund
and rOund and rOund…
and rOund."